HTML JAVA </>

THIS BOOK BELONGS TO:

C++

PHP

_____

THIS BOOK IS DEDICATED TO ALL THE ENGINEERS AND FUTURE ENGINEERS.

C#

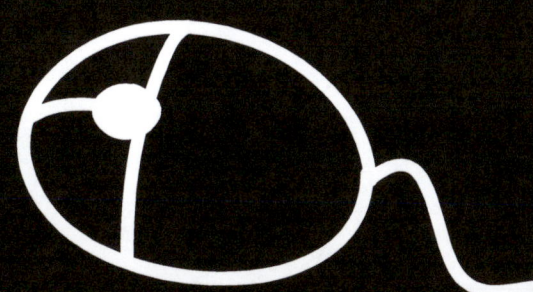

This book is dedicated to my children - Mikey, Kobe, and Jojo.

Copyright © 2024 Grow Grit Press LLC. All rights reserved. No part of this book may be reproduced in any form without permission in writing from the publisher. Please send bulk order requests to info@ninjalifehacks.tv

Paperback ISBN: 978-1-63731-997-0
Hardcover ISBN: 978-1-63731-999-4
eBook ISBN: 978-1-63731-998-7

Printed and bound in the USA.
NinjaLifeHacks.tv

Ninja Life Hacks®
by Mary Nhin

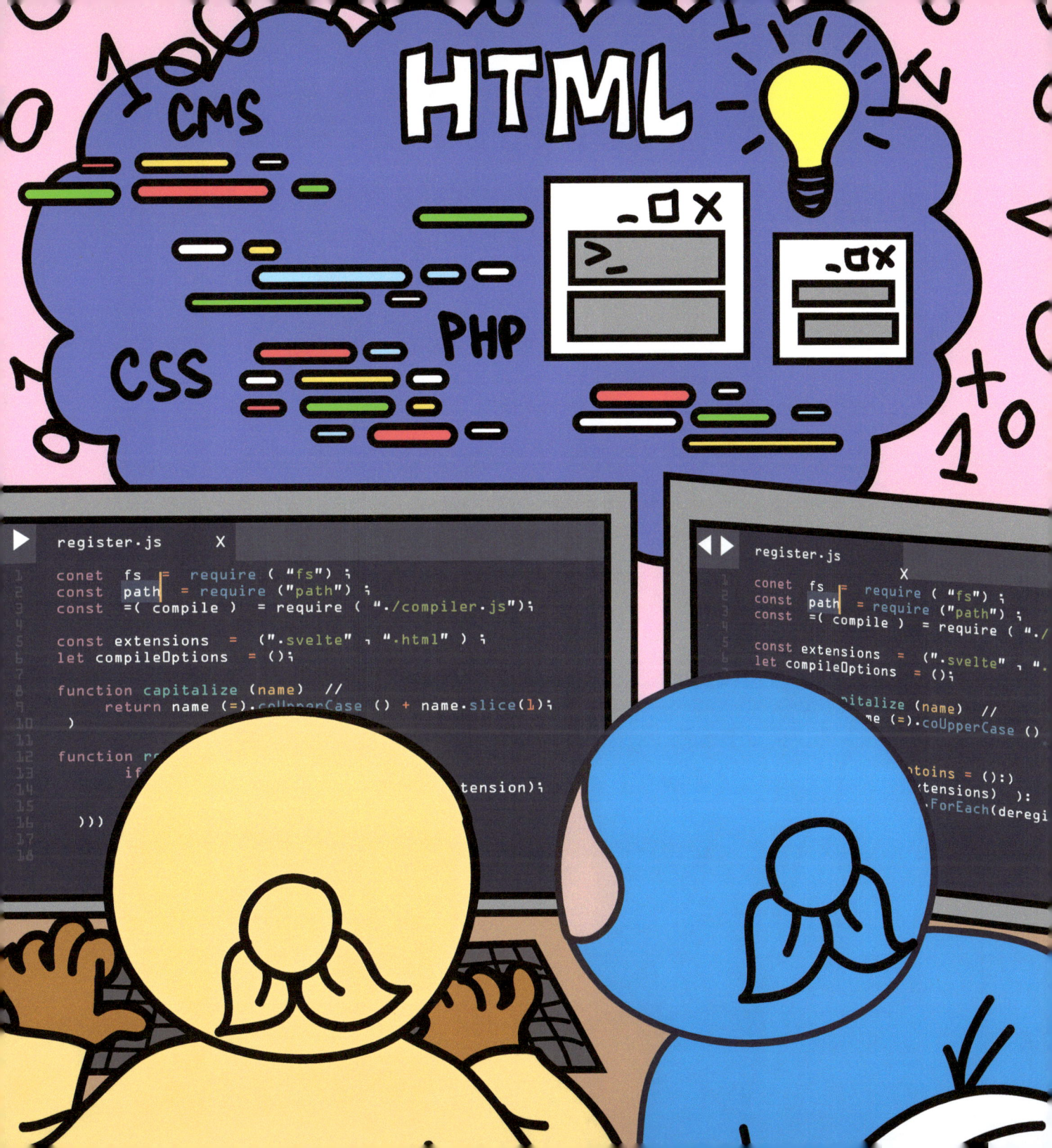

We tested, fixed, and tried once more
With focus sharp and clear.
The app was back, better than before,
As users started to cheer.

So if your update seems to flop,
And bugs make you feel blue,
Just take a breath and work with care,
Patience will see you through.

Check out the fun Coding Ninja lesson plans at ninjalifehacks.tv

I love to hear from my readers. Email me your feedback or thoughts on what my next story should be at info@ninjalifehacks.tv   Yours truly, Mary

 @marynhin   @GrowGrit
#NinjaLifeHacks

 Ninja Life Hacks

 Mary Nhin   Ninja Life Hacks

 @officialninjalifehacks

Design Your Own App

Objective: Today, you're going to design your very own app, just like Coding Ninja! You get to choose the colors, buttons, and even what the app will do. Ready? Let's go!

Supplies needed:

- Paper (white or colorful)
- Markers, crayons, or colored pencils
- Stickers or stamps (optional)
- Glue (optional)
- Scissors (ask for an adult's help with these!)

Instructions:

1. **Design Your App**: Grab your paper and start by drawing your app's screen. Here's what you'll need to include:
   - **App Name**: Come up with a fun name for your app. Make it cool, funny, or totally unique!.
   - **Buttons**: Draw the buttons your app will have. Maybe a play button, a game button, or something special that only your app can do.
   - **Colors and Decorations**: Make it colorful! Use bright colors and feel free to add stickers or stamps to make your app really pop.

2. **What Does Your App Do?**: Now, think about what your app will do. Is it a game? A learning tool? Something super imaginative that no one's ever seen before? Write it down or tell someone about your idea.

4. **Show Off Your App!**: Let's have a mini "show and tell." Share your app with the group, tell everyone what it does, and show off the awesome design you created!

Fix the Glitch - Coding Challenge

Objective: Now it's time to dive into coding, just like Coding Ninja had to fix that glitch! Ready to solve some puzzles and code your way to success?

Supplies needed:

- A coding challenge sheet (your teacher or parent will give you one)
- Crayons or markers
- Optional: Puzzles or mazes related to coding

Instructions:

1. **Start the Coding Challenge!**: On your coding sheet, you'll see a puzzle or maze where you need to follow arrows or symbols to "code" your way through. Use your markers or crayons to color in the arrows and find the right path.

2. **Fixing the Glitch!**: If you spot a mistake or problem on your sheet, be like Coding Ninja and fix it! Color or mark the right parts to solve the puzzle.

3. **Let's Talk About It!**: Coding is all about solving problems and being patient. When you're done, let's talk about how you fixed the glitch and what you learned. Who else fixed it in a different way?

www.ingramcontent.com/pod-product-compliance
Lightning Source LLC
Chambersburg PA
CBHW041713160426
43209CB00018B/1820